DIXIE O'DAY

and the Great Diamond Robbery

Written by
Shirley Hughes

Illustrated by
Clara Vulliamy

THE BODLEY HEAD
LONDON

for Ed,
with love from
Shirley and Clara

Contents

 Chapter One 1

 Chapter Two 19

 Chapter Three 33

 Chapter Four 51

 Chapter Five 63

 Chapter Six 69

Chapter Seven 89

. . . and lots more for you to find!

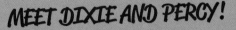

MEET DIXIE AND PERCY!

Dixie O'Day is always ready for adventure, as is his good friend, Percy. And where better to find adventure than on holiday! We quizzed Dixie and Percy about their holiday triumphs and disasters . . .

Hello, Dixie and Percy – thank you for talking to us. First tell us about your perfect holiday.

DIXIE: *That would be staying at the Hotel Splendide in Brightsea, strolling along the beach and getting plenty of fresh sea air.*

PERCY: *Oh yes, with ballroom dancing in the evening . . .*

And who would be your perfect holiday companion?

DIXIE: *Percy and I have had our ups and downs, but I can't imagine a holiday without him.*

PERCY: *I second that!*

What about the worst holiday you've ever had?

DIXIE: *When we were young, we went on a school trip and Percy lost his suitcase. I had to lend him my spare pyjamas!*

PERCY: *It was pretty awful when you were sick on the coach too.*

What do you *always* pack in your suitcase?

DIXIE: *My hot-water bottle, a choice of smart ties and my copy of* 100 Country Walks.

PERCY: *Plenty of chocolate.*

Which do you prefer – the seaside or the mountains?

DIXIE: *The seaside. I don't want to risk engine trouble on the steep mountain roads.*

PERCY: *Me too. Candyfloss on the pier and a trip on a pedalo!*

And finally, is there anything worse than getting sand in your sandwiches?

DIXIE: *Having your tent blown away in the night.*

PERCY: *Arriving too late for supper and finding the hotel dining room closed.*

We agree – that sounds awful. Thank you, Dixie and Percy!

Mr Canteloe
likes:
walking by the sea
stargazing
playing chess

Peaches Miaow
likes:
jewellery
singing
limousines

Detective Inspector Sharply
Chief Inspector for Brightsea Police

Stripy Sid & Alley the Claws
Shady characters

Peaches Miaow's entourage includes:
her manager
her secretary
her press agent
her hairdresser
and her personal trainer

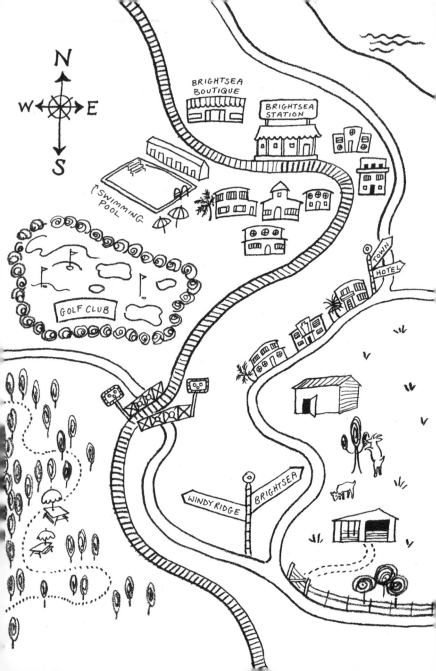

Chapter One

DIXIE O'DAY

One fine summer morning Dixie O'Day said to his friend Percy: 'I've decided it's time to take a little trip. Would you accompany me, Percy?'

'You bet,' said Percy. 'Shall we take the tent and go camping?'

'No, I'm thinking of something a bit more luxurious. I'm booking us in at the Hotel Splendide at Brightsea!'

DIXIE O'DAY

'The Hotel Splendide! That's one of the very poshest hotels on the coast! Won't it be terribly expensive?'

'Never mind that,' Dixie replied nonchalantly. 'I've been saving up for a long while now, and it's time we had a bit of a treat.'

'I'd better pack my bow tie,' Percy said.

'Oh, yes,' said Dixie. 'And of course
we will have to take our dinner jackets
to change into in the evening.'

'Oh dear!' said Percy. 'I only have
the one that belonged to my Uncle Gus!
I'm afraid it's a bit motheaten, and
there are a couple of gravy stains . . .'

'Never mind. Give it a bit of a sponge over, Percy, and you'll look fine. Don't forget you're one of the best ballroom dancers I know – why, you've even won competitions!'

'I'll do my best not to let you down,' said Percy bravely.

They both set to work to give
Dixie's car a good clean, and polished
the bodywork until it shone.

7

DiXiE O'DAY

It was not long before they were driving happily towards Brightsea. They had chosen a quiet side road, which had more scenic views than the motorway and very little traffic.

They were cruising happily along, when suddenly another car zoomed up behind them, seemingly out of nowhere and travelling at reckless speed.

It followed closely, almost touching
their back bumper, then pulled out
and shot past them with inches
to spare. There might have been
a disastrous crash if Percy hadn't
reacted instantly by wrenching the
steering wheel over.

DIXIE O'DAY

They shot up a bank at the side of the road and came to a jolting stop, narrowly missing the fence.

The other car was already roaring away into the distance.

They sat for a while, stunned with shock.

'That was a narrow escape!'
muttered Dixie.

'Demons! Road hogs!' shouted
Percy furiously. 'Did you see their
number plate?' he asked.

and the Great Diamond Robbery

'No, worse luck. I was too busy trying to get out of their way. All I saw was a driver and one passenger. They both had scarves pulled up so you couldn't see their faces properly.'

17

'No good trying to report them for dangerous driving then,' said Percy. 'They should be fined or sent to prison! It's a DISGRACE!'

They carried on with their journey at a careful pace, feeling very upset.

Chapter Two

DIXIE O'DAY

They soon cheered up when they
saw the Hotel Splendide. It was very
grand indeed, high up on a cliff
overlooking the sea.

A man in a smart uniform with many gold buttons stood at the main entrance.

When Dixie and Percy drew up,
he glanced down his nose at Dixie's
car, which was now covered in dust
and mud, and said, 'You'll find a
parking space round at the back, sir.
Do you need someone to help with
your baggage?'

'No thanks, we can manage,' Dixie
answered as casually as he could.

DIXIE O'DAY

Most bedrooms of the Hotel
Splendide were impressively large.

But Dixie and Percy's room was
small and on the top floor at
the back, overlooking
the car park.

As soon as they had
unpacked and made
themselves look as
smart as possible,
they went downstairs.

They found the hotel lobby
full of people. TV reporters, press
photographers and hotel staff were
bustling about everywhere. 'What's
happening?' Percy asked a waiter
scurrying past.

'We're expecting a very important
guest, sir,' he replied. 'The pop star –
Peaches Miaow!'

27

DIXIE O'DAY

As they were speaking, a huge white limousine drew up outside and Peaches herself made a dramatic entrance.

She was followed by her manager, secretary, press agent, hairdresser and personal trainer.

DIXIE O'DAY

'Peaches Miaow!' gasped Percy.
'I've been a fan of hers for years . . .
Thank heavens I remembered to pack
my best bow tie!'

Dixie was unimpressed. And he
was very put out when a pushy press
photographer told him to get out of
the way because he wanted to take a
picture.

Peaches posed briefly in a blaze of
camera flashes, then the crowd parted
to allow her to sweep into the lift and
disappear.

DIXIE O'DAY

'What a fuss!' said Dixie. 'Let's get out of here and take a walk, Percy.'

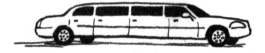

Chapter Three

DIXIE O'DAY

Dixie and Percy scrambled down the cliff path, which brought them onto the beach. It was high tide and a brisk wind was blowing, making the waves choppy.

'Ah, fresh air!' said Dixie,
breathing deeply. 'This is more like
it! Let's take a walk along the jetty.'

DIXIE O'DAY

There were very few people about because everyone had gone up to the Hotel Splendide, hoping to catch a glimpse of Peaches Miaow. As they set off along the jetty, they could see only one solitary gentleman walking far out ahead of them.

DIXIE O'DAY

Spray from the incoming tide flew up and drenched them as they struggled along, heads down against the wind.

They were a good distance from the shore when Percy anxiously clutched Dixie's arm and pointed. The gentleman ahead of them had disappeared!

They ran as fast as they could to the spot where they had last seen him and peered into the sea below. They saw him struggling in the waves. He had been blown over the side, and was hanging desperately on to the bottom rung of an iron ladder. His faint cries for help were lost in the high wind.

DIXIE O'DAY

Dixie reacted immediately.
He stripped off his jacket and
made his way down the ladder.

Once he slipped and nearly lost his footing, but managed to save himself. Percy followed cautiously, close behind.

Now the gentleman
was thrashing
about in the waves.

Every so often he
disappeared altogether . . .

. . . then came
up again,
gasping for air.

Percy grasped the back of
Dixie's trouser belt and
hung on for dear life.
Dixie, clinging to the
ladder with one
hand, reached
out as far as
he dared with
the other.

45

DIXIE O'DAY

Twice he managed to grasp the gentleman by the arm, and twice he slipped away. Then at last their hands met and Dixie pulled with all his might.

Now he had the gentleman by both arms, and, with a huge effort, managed to yank him up onto the bottom rung of the ladder, where they both hung, gulping and spewing up seawater.

DIXIE O'DAY

'You have saved my life!' the
gentleman said, when (sometime later)
all three of them were safely back
on the jetty, recovering a little and
wringing out their wet clothes.

and the Great Diamond Robbery

'I am not a strong swimmer, and without your bravery I would almost certainly have drowned.'

When they parted, he shook them both warmly by the hand, and asked for their names and where they were staying.

Chapter Four

DIXIE O'DAY

Dixie and Percy were in the hotel
lounge, where afternoon tea was
being served, when a letter arrived
from the gentleman they had saved
from drowning.

He introduced himself as Mr Gerald Canteloe, thanked them again and invited them to lunch the following day at his house just across the bay.

'Of course we must accept,' said Dixie. 'It will be interesting to meet him again in more pleasant circumstances.'

That evening
they were both tired.
Dixie wanted to go to
bed early, but Percy
insisted on staying up
to see Peaches Miaow
sweep into the hotel
dining room wearing a
silver satin dress and
a smile as dazzling as
her diamond necklace.
'She looks like a
princess!' whispered
Percy.

'She certainly knows how to make an entrance,' said Dixie dryly. 'Those diamonds must be worth a fortune!'

The next morning they set out to walk to Mr Canteloe's house. It was a lovely old place overlooking the sea.

After an excellent lunch he showed
them the turret where he kept his
telescope for gazing at the stars.

Then he took them downstairs,
through the kitchen to the cellar,
where there was a heavy door,
securely locked and barred.

'This house was once used by smugglers,' he told them. 'Beyond this door is a secret passage which leads to a cave in the cliffs. That's where those rascals used to stash forbidden goods, smuggled in at night by boat.

At high tide it's completely cut off and very damp, so we can't go down there now. But if you would like to see it, come over again tomorrow evening!'

DIXIE O'DAY

'This visit has turned out to be a great deal more eventful than we expected,' said Dixie as they strolled back to the hotel.

'Maybe we'll find some treasure!' said Percy.

Chapter Five

DIXIE O'DAY

That night Dixie could not get to sleep. He lay awake for a long time thinking over the day's events and listening to Percy's snores. The hotel was very quiet.

ZZZ ZZZ ZZZ ZZZ

Peaches – My Life!

100 COUNTRY WALKS

and the Great Diamond Robbery

But then he thought he heard a faint sound – a scratching noise that seemed to be coming from the roof overhead. He listened. It stopped, then came again.

DIXIE O'DAY

He got out of bed and tiptoed to the open window. The car park below, brightly lit by security lights, was deserted. He craned out and looked up, but he could see nothing. He waited, cocked his head, listening intently. But now the noise had stopped altogether.

'Seagulls, I suppose,' he muttered. Then he drew the curtains tight, scampered back into bed, pulled the covers over his head and fell into a deep sleep.

Chapter Six

Next morning Dixie and Percy
came down late for breakfast to find
the hotel in an uproar. Police cars
were parked outside and a crowd
of agitated guests were gathered in
the lobby. In the middle of it all was
Peaches Miaow, having hysterics.

DIXIE O'DAY

'Whatever has happened?' Dixie asked the receptionist.

'I'm afraid there was a robbery last night, sir,' she replied.

'A great many valuables were taken, including Miss Miaow's diamond necklace. Two cat burglars managed to get in through a window without waking the guests.

Luckily someone spotted them
as they were making their getaway.
The Brightsea Police gave chase, but
unfortunately they lost them.'

'Scoundrels!' exclaimed Percy.
'Poor Peaches! What a terrible
experience for her!'

'I thought I heard someone on the
roof last night,' said Dixie, 'but I put
it down to seagulls.'

DiXiE O'DAY

That evening they were only too relieved to escape the turmoil at the hotel and walk over to Mr Canteloe's house again, where he welcomed them, eager to hear all the news about the robbery.

Then he produced two big old-fashioned keys and led them down to the cellar. A dank, musty smell greeted them as he unlocked the door to the secret passage, which swung open.

Shining his torch, Mr Canteloe
went ahead down a narrow flight
of stairs, slimy with damp. Dixie
followed closely behind him. Percy
came last, tightly clutching the back
of Dixie's jacket.

The stairs soon gave way to a passage roughly cut out of the rock, sloping steeply downwards. In some places the ceiling was so low they had to make their way along bent double.

By now they could feel the tang of cold sea air. Then the slope flattened out and they found they were walking on sand and pebbles. They could hear the wash of the tide outside.

They had just reached the cave when Mr Canteloe's torch suddenly cut out, and they were plunged into darkness, broken only by a faint glimmer of moonlight ahead.

'Sorry – the battery's failed,' said
Mr Canteloe.

'I don't like it here,' whispered Percy,
holding onto Dixie more tightly.

'It's all right – just follow me!'

They inched forward and the passage opened up into a cavernous space around them. As they moved into the cave, they heard a scuffling sound and stealthy footsteps. They were not alone!

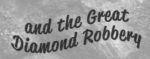

For a moment they stood stock
still. As their eyes adjusted to the dim
light, they looked around and saw
two figures crouching over something
half buried in the sand.

Dixie stepped forward.

'Who are you? What do you want?' he called out, his voice brave and steady.

There was a pause. The figures straightened up and looked towards them. The friends could see two pairs of eyes, glittering in the dark.

Then the figures sprang at Dixie,
making for the entrance to the cave.
Dixie grappled with one of them for
a moment, but the intruder wrenched
free. Dixie tried to clutch at their
sleeve, but there was a ripping sound
as he missed his footing
and fell heavily backwards
into a puddle.

As his two friends ran to his aid,
the intruders seized their chance
to escape. With a rush of scurrying
movement, they were off, splashing
through the shallow water at the
mouth of the cave and on up the
deserted beach.

The three friends chased after
them, slithering on loose pebbles,
vaulting over breakwaters, often
tripping over in the dark. Poor Mr
Canteloe ran bravely but he was
heaving for breath, and Percy's legs
were too short for him to keep up.

The fugitives were too fast for
them. They ran effortlessly, and
seemed to be able to see in the dark.
In no time they had disappeared into
the sand dunes and were gone.

As the three friends went back into
the cave, Mr Canteloe nearly tripped
over something. Looking down, he
saw packages wrapped in plastic bags
strewn about the cave floor.

'Whatever . . . ?' he began.

But Dixie had spotted something else. It was the sleeve which he had ripped from the arm of the intruder's shirt during their struggle, now lying in a puddle. He picked it up and put it into his pocket, and then . . .

DIXIE O'DAY

... there was a loud cry from Percy!

He had found something too, lying half hidden in the pebbles: something which sparkled even in the dim light. He grabbed it and held it up in triumph.

A diamond necklace!

Chapter Seven

It was Peaches Miaow's necklace all right! And when they swiftly set to work opening the packages, they found that they were full of all sorts of other valuables.

Mr Canteloe said: 'These were
almost certainly stolen from the hotel
last night. Those crooks must have
hidden their loot in the cave and
were coming back to collect it when
the coast was clear.'

DIXIE O'DAY

'Thank heavens you spotted Miss Miaow's necklace, Percy!' said Dixie. 'It might have been lost for ever, washed away by the tide. We must return it at once and notify the police!'

They caused a great sensation when they arrived back at the hotel, just as the sun was rising, carrying the stolen valuables. A huge cheer went up from the guests. Detective Inspector Sharply, who was in charge of the case, congratulated them and shook them warmly by the hand.

DIXIE O'DAY

At that moment a police car tore up to the main entrance of the hotel, sirens blazing.

Two police officers got out, and marched a couple of handcuffed suspects into the foyer. They were both struggling and hissing horribly.

'We arrested them for dangerous driving while trying to leave Brightsea,' explained one of the police officers, 'and we think there may be other charges.'

DIXIE O'DAY

Inspector Sharply turned to Dixie and Percy.

'Do you recognize these suspects?' he asked.

'Yes! They are the two rogues we discovered in the cave with all these valuables,' Dixie told them. 'I can prove it!'

And he pulled the sleeve from his
pocket.

'I ripped this off before they both
ran away!'

It was an exact match.

DIXIE O'DAY

'These two suspects are well
known to us as Alley the Claws
and Stripy Sid,' said D. I. Sharply.
'They are suspected of committing
robberies all along the coast. Now we
have evidence to bring them to trial.'

Just then Peaches Miaow rushed down the stairs.

'My necklace is safe at last!' she cried. 'I thought I would never see it again! Oh, thank you, thank you!' And she threw her arms around Percy and kissed him. Percy was quite overcome.

When things had calmed down
a little, Dixie took Mr Canteloe's
arm and led him outside to a quiet
spot overlooking the sea. They sat
in silence for a while, looking at the
incoming tide.

'It's good to have a little peace and quiet at last,' said Dixie. 'That's what we came here for, after all.'

'I hope you'll come and visit us again when things are back to normal,' Mr Canteloe replied.

'You are most kind,' said Dixie, 'although I think next time we take a break we might try somewhere inland.'

DIXIE O'DAY

The manager of the hotel and all his staff were in the lobby to see Dixie and Percy off when they departed the following morning.

'It's been an honour to have you here, sirs,' he said. 'It was entirely through your courage that Miss Miaow's necklace and all the other valuables were found and returned. The reputation of the hotel has been saved. Please come back and visit us again soon – free of charge, of course!'

The doorman snapped his fingers to summon one of the staff to bring Dixie's car round to the front entrance, and put their luggage in the boot.

'We've had it cleaned and polished for you, sir,' he said. 'And may I say what a great pleasure it is to see a car like yours on the road these days.'

DIXIE O'DAY

'Well, it turned out all right in the end,' said Dixie as they set off on the coast road towards home.

But Percy was not listening. He was in a dream, clutching a large framed photograph of Peaches Miaow to his chest.

DIDSWORTH 23

It was signed: 'To Percy – my hero! With love and kisses from Peaches Miaow.'

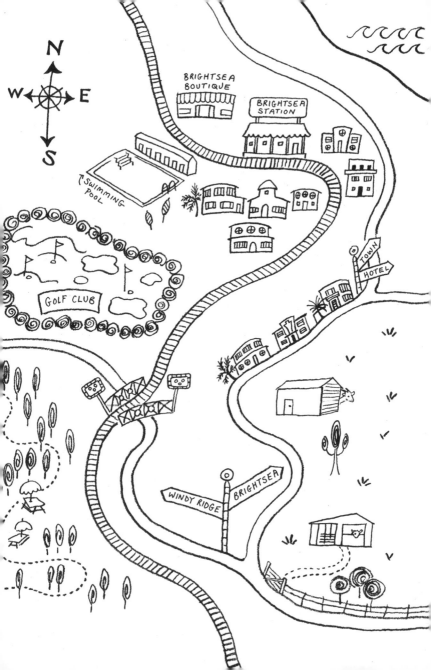

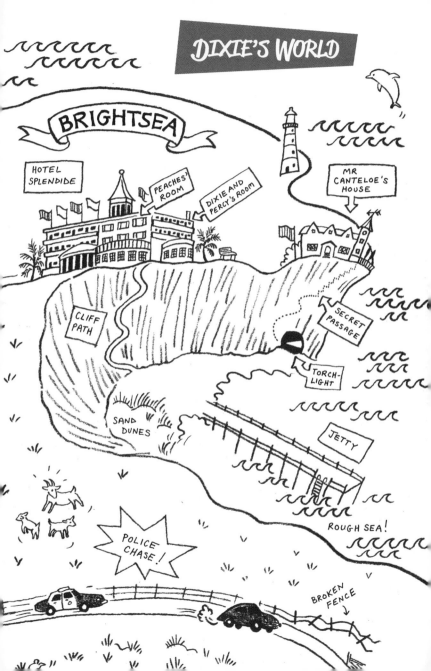

AND NOW MEET
Shirley Hughes and Clara Vulliamy

Shirley is Clara's mum, and together they have created Dixie and Percy's adventures. We thought we'd ask them about their favourite holidays . . .

Hello, Shirley and Clara!
Can you tell us about your perfect holiday?

Shirley: Mine would be with friends and family in a peaceful spot, quite near to home.

Clara: And mine would be a winter holiday with plenty of snow.

And who would be your perfect holiday companion?

Shirley: Clara.   **Clara:** Mum!

What's the worst holiday you've ever had?

Shirley: In a primitive cottage with an outdoor toilet and lots of spiders.

Clara: When I capsized in a canoe without having packed a dry change of clothes.

What do you always pack in your suitcase?

Shirley: My sketchbook.

Clara: My Classic Cars magazines.

What do you like to do on your holiday?

  Shirley: Sunbathe, visit art galleries, lurk about with my sketchbook.

  Clara: Eat an ice-cream sundae, play crazy golf and speed along on a zip-wire (but not all

    at the same time).

And finally, is there anything worse than getting sand in your sandwiches?

  Shirley: Being marooned at an airport with my flight indefinitely delayed.

  Clara: Finding myself in a field with an angry bull.

  YIKES! Thank you so much, Shirley and Clara.

Mysterious Maze

Dixie, Percy and Mr Canteloe
need to rescue the missing loot before
Stripy Sid and Alley the Claws get their paws on it!

Help them find their way through the maze with your finger

and get to the stolen valuables in time!

Now draw a **WANTED** poster of your own dastardly villain!
What is their name, and what do they look like?
Go to **www.dixieoday.com** to find out how to send
your pictures to Dixie and Percy!

The Dixie O'Day Quiz

Dixie has written a special quiz to test you! How much can you remember about **Dixie O'Day and the Great Diamond Robbery?**

1. Who did Percy's dinner jacket once belong to?

2. What's on the number plate of the black car that forces Dixie off the road?

3. What colour is Peaches Miaow's limousine?

4. True or false: Peaches Miaow travels with her hairdresser.

5. True or false: Mr Canteloe rescues Dixie from the sea.

6. What is Mr Canteloe's first name?

7. What book is Percy reading at the Hotel Splendide?

8. How many burglars are there?

9. What does Dixie rip off one of the burglars?

10. True or false: Dixie finds Peaches' necklace in the cave.

11. What does Peaches Miaow give to Percy?

12. On the map of Brightsea, what is next door to the station?

If you enjoyed

DIXIE O'DAY

and the

Great Diamond Robbery

then you'll love Dixie and Percy's

next adventure

DIXIE O'DAY
Up, Up and Away!

Turn over for the first chapter . . .

DIXIE O'DAY
Up, Up and Away!

Chapter One

Dixie O'Day was very proud of his car. He cleaned and polished it every weekend and his friend Percy came to help. One Saturday, when they were giving it an extra shine, Dixie said:

'This is a really good car, but one day I'd like to try a different form of transport.'

'It still goes well,' said Percy encouragingly. But he added, 'As long as you don't try to overtake in the fast lane.'

Dixie's car had given them trouble recently when, during a slow crawl home from the shops, the engine had failed during a traffic jam and he and Percy had ended up pushing it all the way home.

Don Barrakan at the garage had repaired it in no time, of course. But even so there were times when Dixie daydreamed about being effortlessly airborne – up, up and away!

Dixie's irritating next-door neighbour, Lou Ella, bought an expensive new car every year. She liked new things: new clothes, new cars, new furniture, and new kitchen cabinets. She even changed her pets quite often. She had already tired of the goldfish because she thought he was boring, and the Siamese cat because he sharpened his claws on the fitted carpet, and the hamster because he kept her awake at night running and running on his little wheel. She had given them all away, one by one.

Now she had bought a parrot,

and she claimed she was teaching him to speak. His name was Ariel.

She had spent a lot of money on a beautiful parrot perch with ladders, bells and swings, which she had placed in the bay window of her house, so that passers-by could see her interesting new pet. And she devoted a lot of time to grooming him, glossing up his feathers and manicuring his claws. Ariel endured this in pained silence. She even took him for rides in her car. But Ariel simply sat silently in the seat beside her.

She was always trying to get him to talk, but Ariel refused to say a word.

Her friends called round to admire him.

'Can he talk?' they asked.

'Oh yes,' Lou Ella answered, 'of course he can. But he's a bit shy in company.'

Privately she went on urging him to speak, but she was not a patient lady.

'Come on, why don't you say something? The man at the pet shop assured me that you were a very good talker. So why don't you say

"Pretty Polly" or "Who's a clever boy, then?" as other parrots do?'

But Ariel remained stubbornly silent, hunched on his perch.

One morning, when Percy was helping Dixie to shore up a bit of collapsing trellis near Lou Ella's garden wall, they saw Ariel pacing restlessly up and down.

'Good morning!' Dixie called out.

And, to his surprise, Ariel answered back: 'Good morning to you, sir!'

'I didn't know you could speak!' said Dixie, in astonishment.

'Of course I can,' Ariel replied.

'But I just don't care for Lou Ella's boring conversation. She keeps trying to make me say silly, pointless things. She doesn't seem to realize that I am a highly educated bird. It's too humiliating! My confidence is getting so low I've almost forgotten how to fly.'

After this they often chatted together over the garden wall when Lou Ella was out. And they soon discovered that Ariel was indeed a very interesting bird, with many hidden talents.

There's excitement in store for
Dixie, Percy and Ariel . . .
The intrepid threesome become friends
and go off on a special day out
to the big Air Show. And before
long they are swept away on an
adventure in the clouds . . .

Find out what happens next in

DiXiE O'DAY
Up, Up and Away!